The Wentletrap Trap

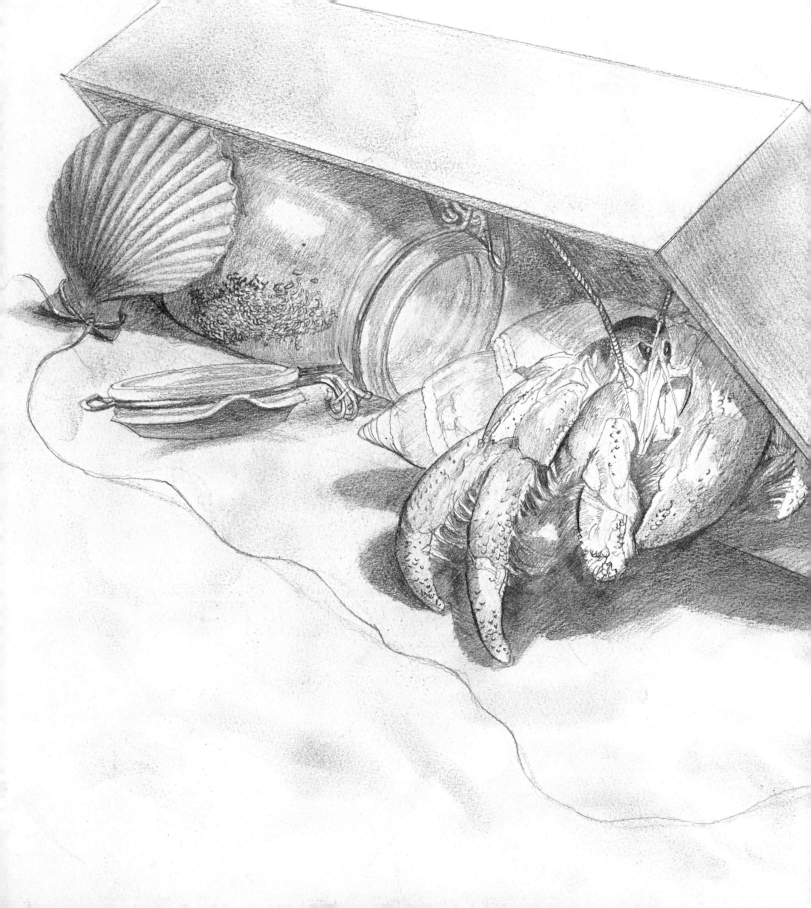

The Wentletrap Trap

Jean Craighead George

pictures by

Symeon Shimin

E. P. Dutton   New York

Library of Congress Cataloging in Publication Data

George, Jean Craighead   The wentletrap trap.

SUMMARY: A young boy living on the island of Bimini
tries to make a trap to catch the rare wentletrap.
[1. Seashore—Fiction.   2. Islands—Fiction]
I. Shimin, Symeon   II. Title.
PZ7.G2933We   [E]   77-4834   ISBN: 0-525-42310-9

Published in the United States by E. P. Dutton, a Division
of Sequoia-Elsevier Publishing Company, Inc., New York
Published simultaneously in Canada by Clarke,
Irwin & Company Limited, Toronto and Vancouver

Editor: Ann Durell

Printed in the U.S.A.   First Edition
10 9 8 7 6 5 4 3 2 1

to Twig George,
who found Dennis and his hermit crabs
on the beach at Bimini
J. C. G.

for Paula, with pleasure
S. S.

Dennis and his father stand on a boat. The boat rocks gently. Red, blue, yellow, and green fish swim in the water.

Dennis and his father live on the island of Bimini. It is a small snip of land in the warm Atlantic Ocean.

"Dennis," says his father, "you must get off the boat now. It's time for me to go to sea."

He picks Dennis up and hugs him. "I must catch plenty of conch to sell to people to use in their soup."

Dennis nods. He knows THAT.

"And while I am gone," his father begins.

"I know what you are going to say," Dennis says. " 'And while I am gone, take good care of yourself.' "

"That's right," says his father, and hugs him again.

Dennis slides down from his arms. He jumps on the dock.

"How can I take care of myself?" he asks. "I don't have a boat or a grapple or a net or a bucket. AND I don't have a fine big hat."

"Man!" says his father, "you need a fortune. You'd better gather a ton of seashells to sell to the tourists."

"How could I carry a ton of seashells?"

"Then you'd better find one wentletrap."

"What is a wentletrap?"

His father leans toward him. "A shell so rare that you can swap it for a boat and a grapple and a net and a bucket. You can even get a hat AND a shelf of new books to give your mother for her classroom in school."

Dennis looks under the dock. "Where do wentletraps live?"

"At the bottom of the sea. They dwell in dark canyons. They drink sea tea and," he pulls up his knee, "they walk on one foot."

"Is that all?" Dennis asks.

"No, they see only two things. They see white. That's the top of the ocean. And black, that's the bottom of the ocean."

"You tease me!" shouts Dennis. "I can't find a wentletrap. I would need a boat and a grapple and a net and a hat even to get near to a wentletrap."

"No, you wouldn't," says his father. "Just watch the beaches. Great storms tear wentletraps loose from the sea bottom. They carry them up on the beaches and leave them there."

Dennis makes a funny face. "And what, sir," he asks, "does this wentletrap look like?"

"It's so white you suck in your breath when you see it. And so beautiful it makes your skin tingle."

The engine roars. The boat moves. Then it speeds out to sea. Dennis stands alone on the dock.

"Oh, Paw," he cries, "I miss you already."

Dennis jumps to the sand. He hides under the dock.

Time passes.

Hiding makes him feel worse.

"I'm not taking good care of myself," he says out loud.

He crawls into the sunlight. He walks slowly home. Soft trade winds blow.

At dawn he awakens. Sea gulls call. A dog barks. Dennis looks out the window. The sky is dark, the sea is white.

"Storm," Dennis says. "Now is the time to catch a wentletrap."

He picks up an empty box. He puts a few tea leaves into a jar. He opens a drawer and takes out a piece of string. Then he picks up a bright silver coin.

Dennis tiptoes to the door.

"Where are you going?" asks his mother.

He jumps in surprise. "I am going to set a trap for a wentletrap."

His mother shakes her head. "Do not stay long. A bad storm is coming."

Dennis walks down the beach. The tide is low. He stares far out at the stormy sea.

"If I were a wentletrap," he says to himself, "and that storm tore me loose, and threw me on shore, what would I do?"

He answers himself. "I would hunt for some sea tea." He puts the jar down on its side next to a conch shell.

"I would look for the sky." He puts the bright coin on the tea jar.

"And I would look for the dark sea bottom." He places the box over the jar.

Then he ties the string to a scallop shell and props the box on the edge of the scallop. He hides himself under a fallen palm leaf nearby. Dennis is ready to trap a rare wentletrap.

He waits and watches.

"Tap. Tap. Tap." The sound comes from the box.

Dennis pulls. The box falls. He lifts it up.

Out walks the tea jar. The jar hurries to the water. The red toes of a hermit crab scutter beneath it.

Dennis shakes his fist. He knows all about hermit crabs. They live inside empty seashells. The hard shells protect their soft bodies from harm. As they grow, the hermit crabs hunt for bigger shells. When they find one, they slide their bodies out of the old shells and into the new shells. And they run on their way.

Dennis is mad. "You took my tea jar!" he yells to the hermit crab. "So I'll take your conch shell for my trap."

He sets the trap again. Tap. Tap. Tap. He looks under the box. A moon shell sits where the conch shell sat. The conch shell is running down to the sea. The toes of another hermit crab scutter beneath it.

"Give me my conch shell!" Dennis roars. But this crab disappears too.

"You took my conch shell, so I'll take your moon shell." Dennis peers under the box. Where the moon shell sat, a cone shell sits.

"Okay," Dennis says to the crabs. "I'll make a hermit-proof wentletrap trap."

He ponders a moment. "If I were a wentletrap, I would *not* want tea. I would *not* look for the sky."

He puts the coin back in his pocket. "But I WOULD want to find my dark home. <u>SO</u> I would slide right under this box."

Dennis props up the box. He watches and waits. The sky grows dark. Thunder rumbles. The wind whips the sea. Lightning flashes.

Dennis runs to his mother. The rain slashes. Thunder cracks and booms. Dennis curls up in his mother's lap.

"Is Paw all right on the stormy sea?"

She holds him tightly. She does not answer.

The storm rumbles and bangs. At last it growls off like a wounded dog. The rain stops. The sun shines. Water drips softly from leaf and flower. A bird calls.

Dennis slides to the floor.

"I must go check my wentletrap trap," he says to his mother.

She smiles.

He runs down the beach. The tide is high. And the wentletrap trap is under the sea.

"BAH!" cries Dennis. "I will never be able to take good care of myself."

"Dennis!" His mother is calling. "Look what I've found!

She runs down the beach and sits beside him. "It's an old bottle the storm washed up."

Dennis holds it. He turns it over. He shrugs. He puts the bottle down on the sand.

"Don't you like it?"

"I need a wentletrap," Dennis says, "to swap for a boat and a grapple and a net and a bucket and a HAT."

His mother looks up. "Well," she says, "the bottle is not worth a boat or a grapple or a net or a bucket. But you just might swap it for a wonderful hat."

She points down the beach. "Here comes Sinclair. He is wearing a new hat that he made to sell to the tourists."

Sinclair strides toward them. On his head is a hat bright with feathers from parrots and peacocks. It is rimmed with red bottle caps. It is hung with bright pop tops. On its crown sits a small wooden teacup and a saucer. The hat is a masterpiece.

Dennis runs to meet Sinclair. "Want to swap your hat for an old purple bottle?"

"Sure," says Sinclair. "I can make a new hat, but not an old bottle."

Dennis runs back to his mother. The bottle is gone! A white shell sits there instead.

Dennis is furious. He stamps the ground. He kicks at the hermit in the shell. Then he sucks in his breath. He feels his skin tingle.

"A wentletrap!" Dennis shouts. "I have a wentletrap!"

He leans over the snowy white shell. "Yippee. Hooray."

He turns a cartwheel. "I can, and I will take good care of myself."

He reaches for the wentletrap. It runs to the sea. A wave falls upon it, and the shell disappears.

"Wave!" shouts Dennis, "bring back my wentletrap. Bring it right back to me!"

The wave does not answer.

Dennis throws himself face down on the sand.

"I can't," he sobs. "I just can't take care of myself."

"You don't have to."

Dennis looks up. His father is here. His hat is tipped back at a happy angle. He is hugging Dennis's mother.

"The storm was so bad," he tells Dennis, "that I took good care of myself. I came back to you."

Dennis leaps to his feet. "Hey, Paw," he says. "Let's take good care of our two selves together."

He runs toward the boat, the grapple, the net, and the bucket. Then he thinks of his father's fine big hat.

Dennis stops.

He picks up a teapot. The storm washed it up. He turns it slowly over and over. Then carefully he puts it on his head. He pushes it back at a happy angle.

"Okay," he says to his laughing father. "It's time for me to go to sea."

They run.

A little red foot sticks out of the pot spout.

When Jean Craighead George was a student at Penn State, she spent part of a Thanksgiving vacation viewing WPA murals at the Justice Department in Washington, D.C. She was struck by the exquisite feeling conveyed by the work of one artist in particular. Standing beside his ladder, she watched him paint.

As editor of her college literary magazine, she asked if he would come to the campus and share his thoughts with the staff. Symeon Shimin accepted. Both of them carried happy memories of the meeting; both were delighted to meet again, many years later, when Mr. Shimin was asked to illustrate *The Wentletrap Trap*.

The mural which won the author's admiration is opposite the entrance to the Attorney General's office. In praising the mural, President Franklin D. Roosevelt cited the compassion it reflects.

The text type is linotype Granjon, and the display type is foundry New Caslon. The illustrations were drawn in pencil, and the book was printed by offset at Halliday Lithographers.

DATE DUE

NOV 3 0 1978	FEB 2 6 1992	
APR 2 1979		
APR 8 1980		
MAR 1 8 1982		
APR 9 1982		
MAR 2 9 1983		
MAY 1 2 1983		
MAY 2 4 1983		
1-10-84		
NOV 2 5 1986		
11/23/86		
APR 3 1988		
MAY 2 1 1988		
1-22-90		
APR 0 2 1991		
FEB 0 6 1992		

GAYLORD   PRINTED IN U.S.A.